Mouse Manual

Written by Jill Eggleton
Illustrated by Kelvin Hawley

CONTENTS

Mouse Hair Dye

What to do:

Step One: Mix dyes with warm water.

Step Two: Stir well.

Step Three: Rub over hair.

Sit in the sun for 4 hours.

Warning:

Do not drink the mix.

Keep the mix away from baby mice.

Cough Mixture

Dose:

Take two sips four times a day.

Shake well.

Warning

Do not take the mix if you have been eating cake crumbs.
Do not give to mice under one year old.

COUGH MIXTURE

MOUSE TRAPS

What to do in an emergency:

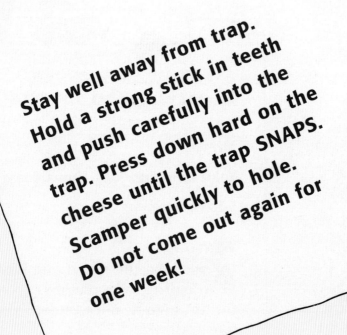

Stay well away from trap. Hold a strong stick in teeth and push carefully into the trap. Press down hard on the cheese until the trap SNAPS. Scamper quickly to hole. Do not come out again for one week!

5

Cheese Balls

Ingredients

- **one small piece of tasty cheese**
- **breadcrumbs**
- **small seeds**

1 Put the cheese on a large leaf. Leave in the sun to melt.

2 Mix in breadcrumbs.

3 Make into small balls.

4 Roll in seeds.

5 Put in a cold place until the cheese balls are hard.

7

M O U S E

C O D E

To send messages, you can use flags:

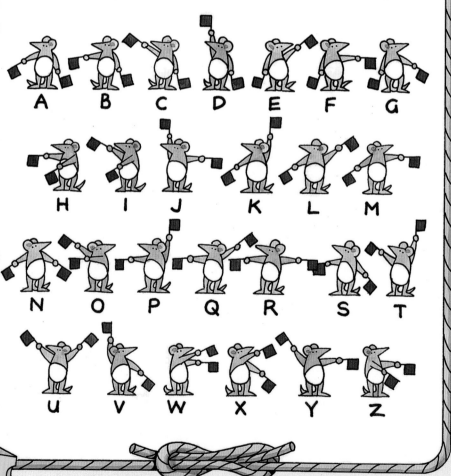

A B C D E F G

H I J K L M

N O P Q R S T

U V W X Y Z

Can you read the message?

--- --- --- --- --- ---

--- --- --- --- ---

--- --- --- --- --- --- ---

Cheese Factory

Mouse

You will need:

- 1 small nut
- 2 sticks
- 2 teams
  (6 mice in each team)

How to Play

1. Mark an oblong on the grass.
2. Put one stick at each end of the oblong for the goals.
3. Make a circle in the middle of the oblong. Put the nut in the middle of the circle for kick-off.

One team kicks the nut off. When the nut goes over the goal stick, the team gets a point. The team with the most goals after ten minutes wins.

Rules

- Don't touch the nut with tails or teeth!
- Don't run with the nut!
- Don't squeak!

Soccer

MOUSE PARACHUTE

You will need:

- a short cardboard tube
- a piece of cardboard
- a piece of thin cloth (20in. long and 20in. wide)
- 4 pieces of yarn (25in. long)
- sticky tape and glue
- scissors

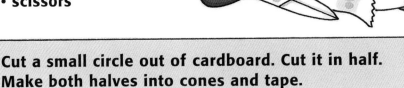

1 Cut a small circle out of cardboard. Cut it in half. Make both halves into cones and tape.

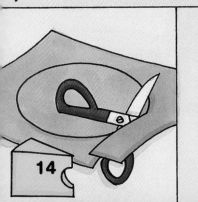

2 Glue the cone to the top of the cardboard tube.

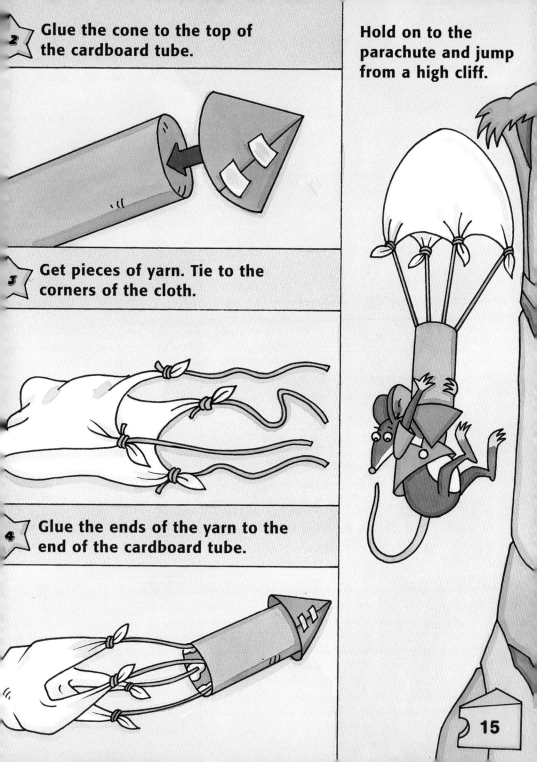

3 Get pieces of yarn. Tie to the corners of the cloth.

4 Glue the ends of the yarn to the end of the cardboard tube.

Hold on to the parachute and jump from a high cliff.

Stick

You will need:

- a stick
- a water hole
- 2 players:
  Mouse One and Mouse Two

What to do:

1. Put the stick in the water.
2. Make sure that it floats.
3. Mouse One stands on one end of the stick.
4. Mouse Two stands on the other end of the stick.
5. Rock the stick until one mouse falls in the water.
6. The mouse who stays on the stick is the winner.

Rules

No holding on to the stick with tails.

Wobbling

MANUALS

Manuals give instructions about:

- how to make something
- how to do something
- how to use something
- how to find something

How to __MAKE__ something

How to __DO__ something

How to __USE__ something

How to __FIND__ something

Before writing instructions, ask:

Why am I writing?
Who am I writing for?
How can I make instructions clear?
What is the best order?
Would diagrams or maps help the reader?

Instructions use verbs

mix, stir, rub, tap, cut, curl, tie, rock

Instructions have steps in order

Step One: Mix dyes with warm water.
Step Two: Stir well.
Step Three: Rub over hair. Sit in the sun for 4 hours.

1. Put the cheese on a large leaf.
   Leave in the sun to melt.
2. Mix in breadcrumbs.

Some instructions have diagrams

Guide Notes

Title: Mouse Manual
Stage: Fluency (1)

Text Form: Manual
Approach: Guided Reading
Processes: Thinking Critically, Exploring Language, Processing Information
Written and Visual Focus: Manual, Instructions, Diagrams, Map

THINKING CRITICALLY
(sample questions)
- What instructions tell you how to do something?
- What instructions tell you how to make something?
- What instructions tell you how to use something or find something?
- If you were going to make cheese balls, what would you have to have first? Why do you think you would have to have this first?
- Look at the instructions on "Mouse Hair Dye." Why do you think the order is important? What might happen if you left out some instructions?

EXPLORING LANGUAGE

Terminology
Spread, author and illustrator credits, ISBN number

Vocabulary
Clarify: manual, ingredients, emergency, code, oblong, tube
Nouns: mouse, hair, hole, cheese, soccer
Verbs: rub, stir, scamper, kick, run, squeak
Singular/plural: sip/sips, trap/traps, seed/seeds, ball/balls

Print Conventions
Apostrophes – contraction (don't)
Colon, bullets